DreamWorks

Trolls

Little Look and Find® BONUS!

5 "Meet the Trolls" bonus activities!

Written by Veronica Wagner

Illustrated by Art Mawhinney

phoenix international publications, inc.

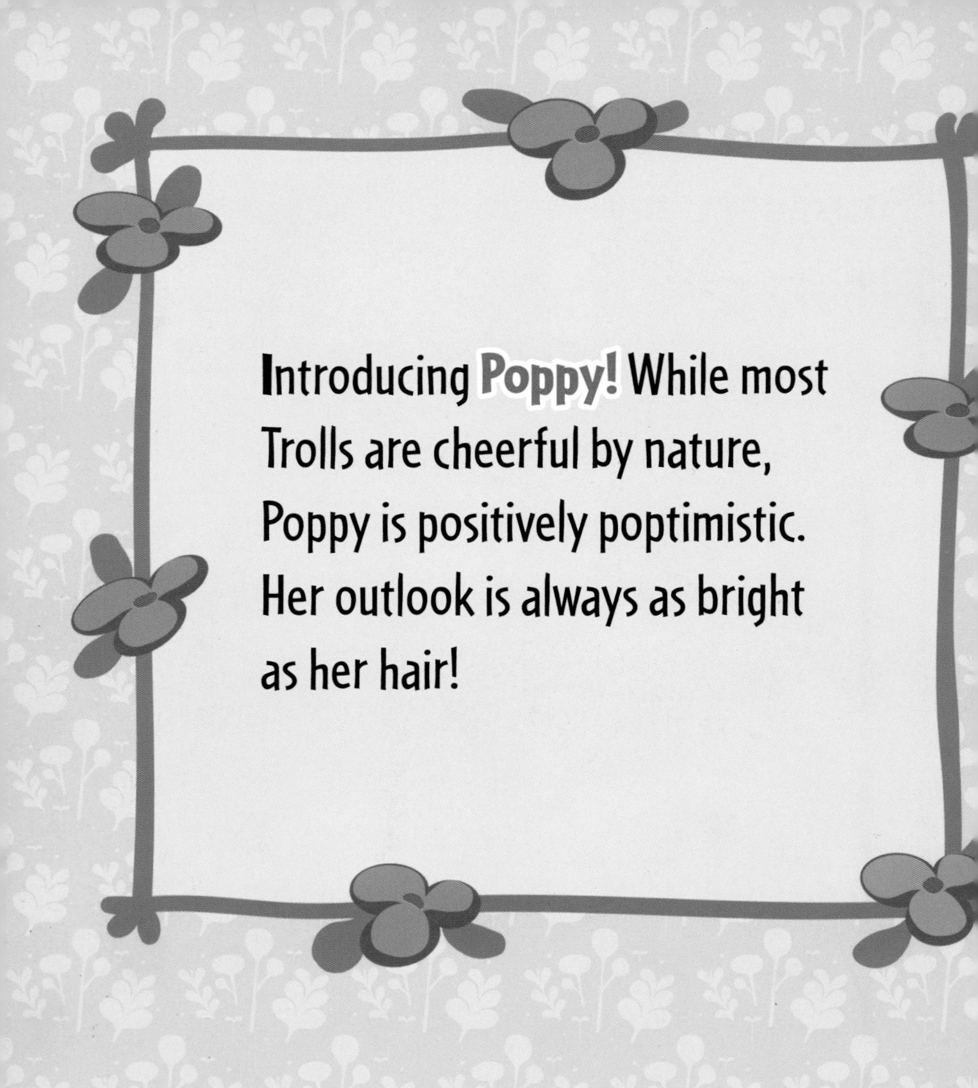

Introducing **Poppy!** While most Trolls are cheerful by nature, Poppy is positively poptimistic. Her outlook is always as bright as her hair!

Ask Poppy and she'll tell you: it's always time for a hug! Can you find **three** differences between these hug stickers?

"Positivity is my super-power!"

Poppy looks forward to the happy day when she will be the Queen of all Troll Village! In the meantime, she's busy keeping her scrapbooks up to date.
Find these mementos in Poppy's book:
TRUE COLORS
color wheel
rainbow patch
baby picture
wrapper from a favorite cupcake
TIME for a
hug sticker
sheet music
PARTY

TRUE COLORS
TIME for a HUG

"Be prepared!"

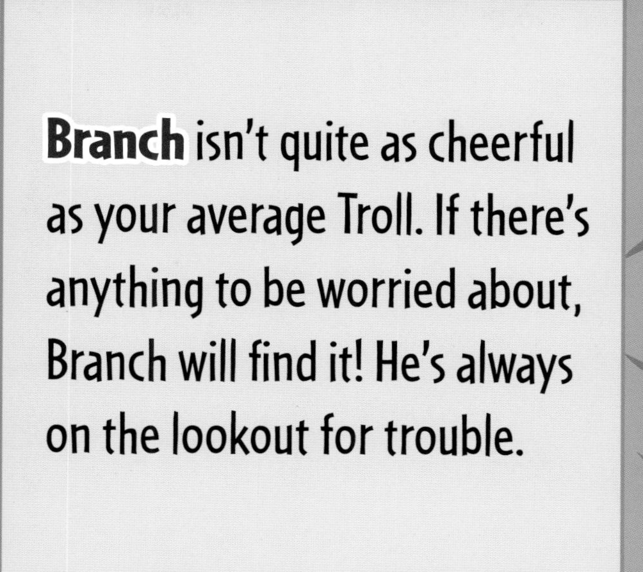

Branch isn't quite as cheerful as your average Troll. If there's anything to be worried about, Branch will find it! He's always on the lookout for trouble.

ch gets invited to a lot of Village parties, even though ever shows up. Noisy parties d attract a Bergen! One of e invitations is different the others. Which one?

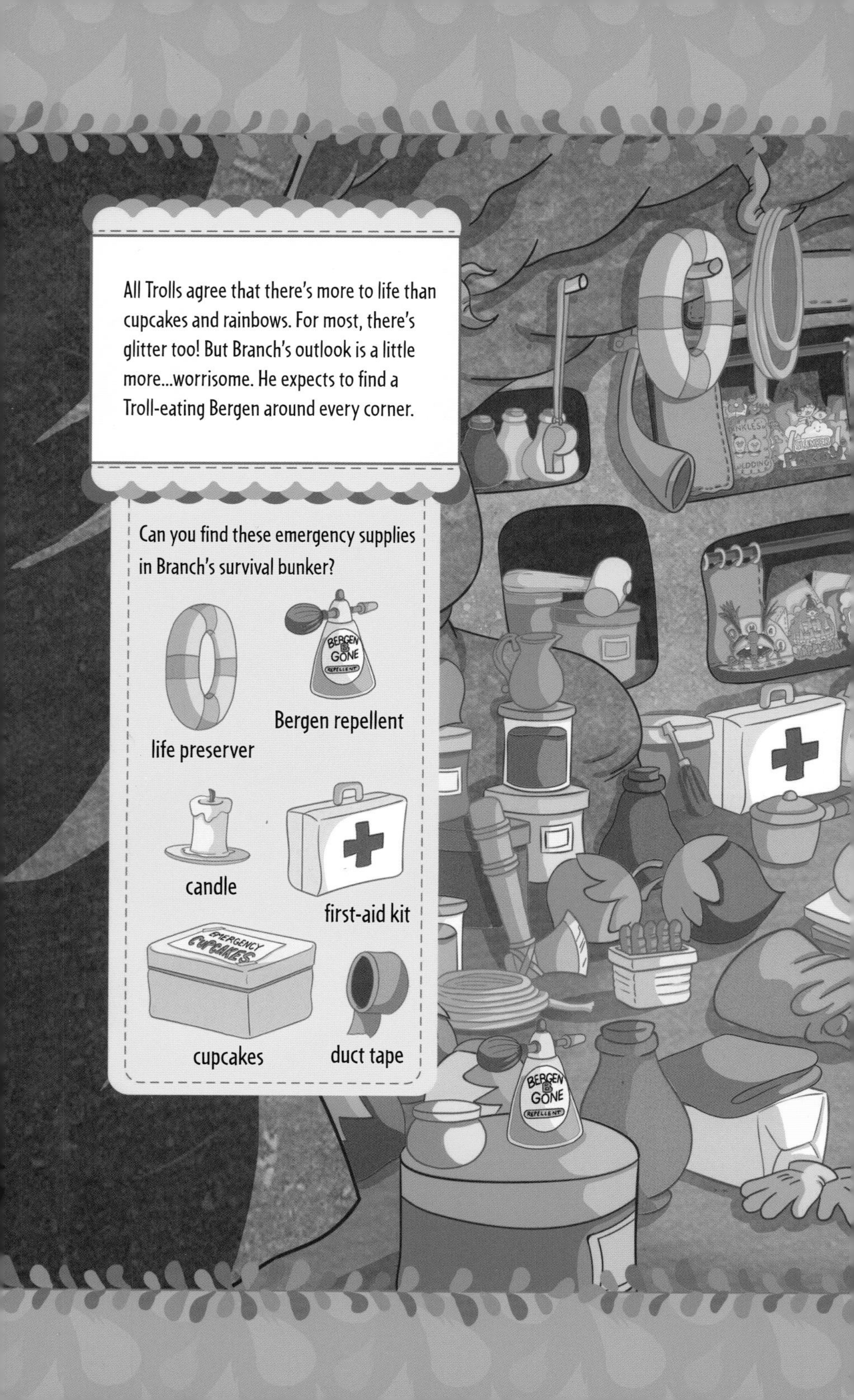

All Trolls agree that there's more to life than cupcakes and rainbows. For most, there's glitter too! But Branch's outlook is a little more...worrisome. He expects to find a Troll-eating Bergen around every corner.

Can you find these emergency supplies in Branch's survival bunker?

life preserver

Bergen repellent

candle

first-aid kit

cupcakes

duct tape

EMERGENCY
CUPCAKES

Want a cupcake? Biggie always does! He's looking for his favorite flavors on the cupcakery's shelves.

Can you help Biggie find these tasty treats?

"Get ready to rock 'n' Troll!"

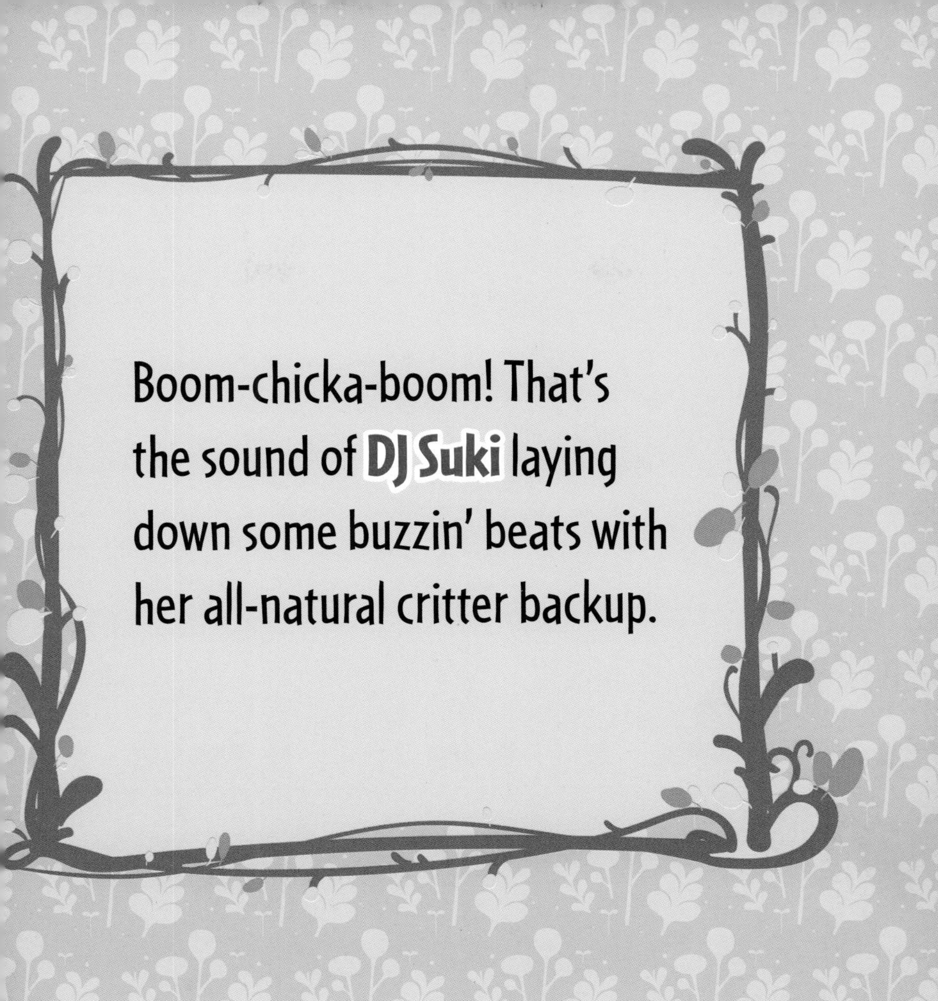

Boom-chicka-boom! That's the sound of **DJ Suki** laying down some buzzin' beats with her all-natural critter backup.

ki's sound depends
er critter chorus!
ou see five differences
een these critters?

DJ Suki is holding auditions for her next critter-inspired music track. She can find the beat in every Skitterboard and the crescendo in every Caterbus!
Can you find these up-and-coming music makers?
this Glowfly
this Caterbus
this Humworm
this Chorusfly
this Glowfly
this Sparkbug

“Does this make my hair look big?”

Satin and Chenille like jewelry. Lots of jewelry! This jewelry box is an exact match to one on the right. Which one?

Meet Troll Village's BFFFs. **Satin** and **Chenille** are not only sisters, they're Best Fashion Friends Forever!

Satin and Chenille may be twins, but they never wear the same outfit at the same time. They're much too creative for lookalike styles!
Can you spot these clothing choices in the closet chaos?
this sock
this belt
jumpsuit
these earrings
this dress
this scarf

King Gristle of Bergen Town would love a slice of Troll pizza. Luckily, it's not on the menu... yet. Gristle will have to be happy with the current selection.
Look around for these peculiar pies:
pickle pizza
hot dog pizza
ice cream pizza
lollipop pizza
fruit pizza
veggie pizza

After twenty years of searching, Chef has finally found the Trolls! She is determined to take them back to Bergen Town...as the centerpiece of her Trollstice dinner menu.
These Trolls are trying to hide from Chef. Can you find them...before she does?
Smidge
Cooper
this Troll child
Fuzzbert
Biggie
King Peppy

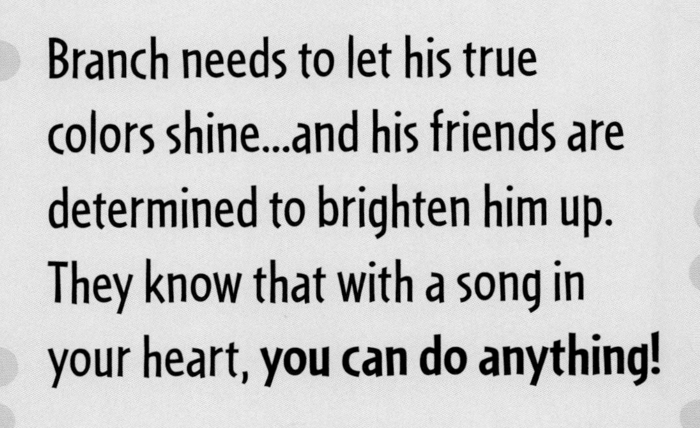

Branch needs to let his true colors shine...and his friends are determined to brighten him up. They know that with a song in your heart, **you can do anything!**

Poppy's devotion to Branch is a reflection of her good nature. Can you spot the Poppy on the right that's an exact duplicate of this one?

"Especially if there's
a cowbell involved."

Poppy and her pals are ready to celebrate what makes each Troll special. The best time to show off your true colors is always...now!
Can you find these colorful components at Poppy's party?
a pink hair bow
this orange hair
this green hat
a yellow jewel
these purple pants
a blue flower

Poppy's coronation daydreams find their way into her scrapbooks too. Turn back to her tome to find these sovereign scribbles:

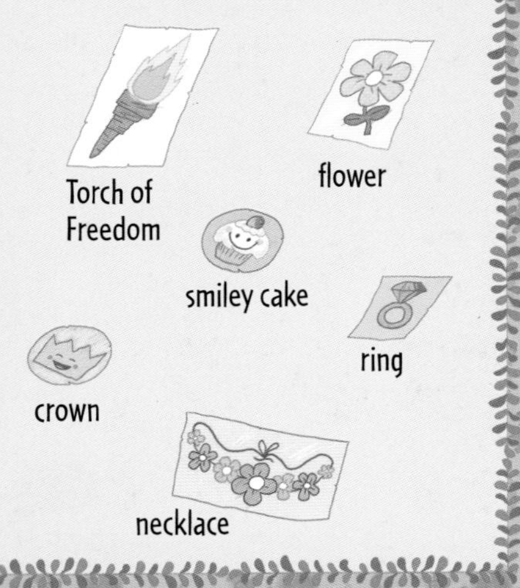

Branch hasn't found his true colors yet. Bu there *are* colors waiting to be found–even his bunker! Bop back to the bunker to find something that is:

Bustle back to Biggie to spot these cupcakery contraptions:

DJ Suki's audition has attracted a sextet of swinging Skitterboards! Shoot back to the sh and find these multi-colored Skitterboard musicians: